Ian Saint-Barbe Anderson

illustrated by

Gabrielle Bordewich

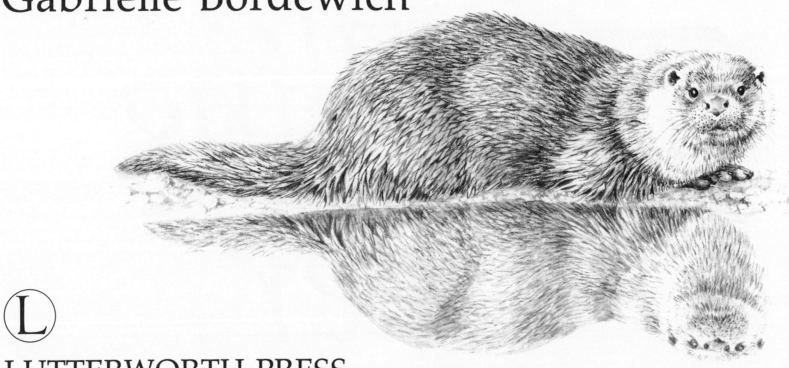

Ⓛ

LUTTERWORTH PRESS
Cambridge, England

A
Travelling
Otter

First published 1985 by
Lutterworth Press
7 All Saints' Passage
Cambridge CB2 3LS

To
our children
Callum and Kate
with love

ISBN 0 7188 2622 1

Printed in Great Britain by
Redwood Burn Ltd, Trowbridge, Wiltshire

Contents

Acknowledgements

My most grateful thanks go first to naturalist David Chaffe, whose otters provided the inspiration for both the story and the drawings in this book. He has allowed my wife Gabrielle and me to spend hours with them over the years. The illustrations of Kestrel, Shag and Tawny Owl are based on David's birds. My knowledge of otters comes in no small part from getting to know his creatures. David Chaffe is only the second person to have bred the European Otter in Britain in the last eighty-five years; there have now been some six successful 'cubbings', and recently a youngster was sent to the Otter Trust where under the auspices of its chairman, Philip Wayre, it has in turn 'fathered' cubs which may eventually be suitable for further release schemes back into the wild. My thanks also go to the Vincent Wildlife Trust who introduced me to David and to otter habitats through my work for them as a photographer. I am also very grateful to Philip Wayre, the leading otter expert in Britain and the chairman of the Otter Trust. The Trust is unique in actively conserving our otters by breeding them for re-release into the wild. I am honoured that he has written the foreword to this book.

I would like to thank Merriel Hake, who allowed us to stay in her cottage in otter territory. It was that experience which triggered this book. From the first day of our stay Gabrielle and I could sense the presence of otters around us.

Finally, my thanks to go Helen Duffey for her invaluable help once again in typing the manuscript.

Ian Saint-Barbe Anderson

Foreword

Persecuted in the past as a destroyer of fish, the otter has inspired authors and artists alike during the present century. By its intelligence, beauty and effortless movement it has evoked a sense of wonder and admiration in all those lucky enough to have watched one in the wild.

Secretive, nocturnal and becoming increasingly rare throughout the whole of western Europe the otter is unlikely to be seen by even the keenest naturalist, but books like this one can do much to arouse public interest in this delightful animal and concern for its future. Pollution of our waterways by agricultural chemicals, sewage effluent and industrial waste, combined with the wholesale drainage of marshes, the canalisation of rivers, the clearing of bankside vegetation and the felling of woodlands have combined to wipe out the otter in possibly forty-one of the fifty-two counties in England and Wales. Now a comparatively recent threat, the eel fyke net, is being used in more and more rivers and lakes and on an increasing scale. These nets with their large funnel entrances are lethal to otters because once inside, attracted by curiosity or by the eels within, the otter is unable to find the way out and soon drowns. The use of such nets by commercial eel fishermen has already wiped out the remaining otters from what was once one of the best rivers in Norfolk. The fate of the few otters remaining in England hangs in the balance unless legislation is passed to ensure that excluders in the form of large mesh grids are fitted to all fyke nets. It would be deplorable if children of a future generation inspired by Ian Anderson's tale had no chance of seeing this wonderful animal, except possibly on some remote Scottish island.

Its quicksilver nature makes the otter an extremely difficult subject for the photographer or artist and few have captured its natural grace and beauty of form in the way that Gabrielle Bordewich has done in her drawings which illustrate her husband's book.

I am privileged to be allowed to express my appreciation of this team effort and delighted that some of the otters here depicted belong to my friend and erstwhile pupil David Chaffe.

Philip Wayre
Chairman, The Otter Trust
Earsham Suffolk

Prologue

In the book, *A Tangle of Otters*, three cubs had been born on the Levels in November. Two of them had not survived the dangers of growing up in the wild, but a sole male cub had come safely through the perilous passage into adult life. The book ended with his mother preparing to start a new family by rejoining her mate. The cub was pushed out into the world, to face life's struggle on his own, and we left him 'about to start his journey into adult life'.

    A Travelling Otter begins at this point.

Chapter One

THE YOUNG DOG OTTER, now nearly eleven months old, and practically full-grown, found himself for the first time in his life completely on his own. He had always enjoyed the rough and tumble of life with his brother and sister, but they were both dead now. His mother's loving attention too had gradually diminished as she prepared him for a life of his own. Her renewed meetings with the big dog otter, his father, had excluded him, forcing him reluctantly to turn away from his parents. He sensed that life was going to be different now.

He remained in the vicinity of his parents for several days more, following their spraint trail, but never hurrying to keep up with them. His father felt like a stranger, and he was not sure how he would be received if he made the effort to catch them up and join them again. He was miserable, and intensely lonely. His mood was echoed by the dull autumn weather. For days the heavily overcast sky had blotted out the sun, and had instead released a slow unceasing drizzle that insinuated its way into every corner of every shelter the young otter sought.

When he hunted, it was only in order to satisfy the dull hunger he felt. He took no pleasure in chasing fish. He wandered through the soggy squelching meadows and ditches of the Levels for days. His normally scrupulously clean coat became mud-spattered and lacklustre. Each afternoon he awoke to grey wet light, and rose wearily to mope in the wake of his parents as they journeyed down river.

On the sixth night of this empty existence he found he had

reached the mouth of the river. Trying unsuccessfully to deaden the ache inside him, he went fishing for his favourite food: eels. He caught two male eels in succession, and ate them with obvious enjoyment. Then he sank back into his lethargy, and aimlessly roamed the mudflats. He picked up his mother's scent, and noted the presence of the big dog otter a moment later. He moved away and swam out into the bay.

Later that night he returned to the flats, and searched for a place to sleep. He investigated an old sea wall, and found a dry ledge which ran back into it. It was a stone drain that had been blocked by earth from the field that it served, and was now dry within.

The otter scrabbled up into it, and found to his surprise that it was not damp. He squeezed his wet fur against the sides of the drain, and moved deep inside it. He curled up in a tight damp ball, and shivered himself into sleep. By first light he was sleeping fitfully. His body trembled as uneasy nightmares invaded his sleep. Then, as the sun touched the wall he dreamed it was summer once more, and that he was warm and dry, basking on a bank, watching his mother fish for him. It seemed the bitch otter was swimming gradually further and further from him, and he was filled with the knowledge that she would continue to do so, until she disappeared forever. He was strangely untroubled in his dream; he felt it was all right, because he was comfortable where he was, warm and dry, and that he would follow his mother later – when he felt more awake. He watched his mother's head bobbing on the waves until it vanished amongst them. As the dream ended, he awoke.

He felt the warmth of the sun still, and the dry stone, and lived on in his dreams for a few moments. Then, seeing a calm sea stretching away before him to the far mountains on the distant shore across the estuary, he felt a great compulsion to follow his mother, across the expanse of water to the beckoning hills beyond.

His sorrow had kindled in him the wanderlust which all otters experience, and which governs their way of life. His recent misery at being an outcast coupled with his intense sense of family loss combined to trigger a new and powerful urge to discover a new range for himself – to start a fresh way of life, alone. Rejected by his mother he knew now that he must make his own way in life.

He suddenly felt purposeful, and stretched in contentment at the warmth of the newly arrived sun. He went to the lip of the cill, and looked out into the calm, still afternoon. Only the slop of

wavelets breaking on mud, and the far-flung, plaintive cry of a gull broke the silence around him. He jumped down on to the mud. He stopped almost at once to listen for danger. Far away noises, from further up the river, reached his ears, but were so distant as to pose no threat to him. It was a balmy autumn afternoon, one of the first in October, and he responded to the change in the weather with a new vigour.

Hunger urged him to go fishing before setting out on his big swim. He caught several eels at the rivermouth, and sated his appetite fully. Then he cleaned himself thoroughly, bathing in the fresh water upstream that was not tainted with the sea's flavour. Next he rolled and rubbed himself on the springy short turf above the beach, in quick lively movements that squeezed all the water out of his fur. He groomed his coat – lifting his head frequently to listen for danger as he did so. Having fully prepared himself, as though to mark his point of departure from his old home ground, he finally climbed on to a large boulder above the tide-line and sprainted on to it.

Without a further backward glance he ran to the sea, and began his big swim. Once in the sea he lost sight of the far mountains, except when a big wave lifted him high on its crest for a moment. He swam steadily, conserving his energy, and made good progress, buoyed up by the salt water. The distance he had to cross was about two miles, and for a while he seemed no closer to the glimpsed mountain range beyond the waves. Then as he covered his first half mile, his progress at last seemed to have tangible form, as he realised the shape of the landscape loomed a little larger now.

His eyesight was better suited to close-range vision, but experience had taught him to interpret the tone and size of the landscape as it impinged on his imperfect vision. His brain supplied the details from its store of experience that his eye lacked. He could in fact 'see' the landscape ahead. Now he could make out the dark tones of the mountains, and as he drew nearer to them he gained a new confidence.

After a while he became aware that the land ahead was changing shape. He also noticed that the water tasted less salty, and did not bear him up so well. He realised he had entered the fresh waters of a river that flowed into the sea. The strength of its current was pushing the salt water aside as it entered the estuary. The otter was being carried down the estuary by the force of the river, which was more powerful than the recently turned incoming tide, now flooding inshore. He swam more urgently, struggling to master the forceful current as it swept him off course. He was tiring, and beginning to panic when he finally realised he had begun to make headway into the far edge of the freshwater race. He gradually found he was lifted higher in the water, and swimming faster again. He tasted the tang of salt once more, and knew the worst of his struggle was over.

As soon as he had cleared the strong current, he rested in the waves, allowing the incoming tide to push him towards the mountains once more. He lay on his back in the water watching the vague shapes of the cloudy sky above him. A layer of rolling, rain-heavy grey clouds straddled the horizon. Above them rose towers of cumulus, reaching high into the pale blue wintry sky.

As the otter lay dozing, a flurry of wind dashed foam from the wave-crests down over him, needling his eyes and pricking him into wakefulness as he blinked at the stinging salt. He rolled over to dip his head into the cold sea, and began to swim once more. As he drew nearer the new shore, a dark shape appeared from behind a wave, very close to him. It flew right over him. He dived at once, and was disconcerted to see the shape enter the water just ahead of him. He was already turning to swim in the opposite direction when he noticed that the object which had entered the water was rapidly disappearing. He changed his mind and bobbed up to the surface. A bird's head popped out of the water close by with a fish in its beak. It was a cormorant, and it had not noticed the otter until they both dived. Now that it saw him so close it rose up with a great lunge, and ran on the water slapping it with webbed feet, wings beating powerfully to lift it clear of the waves. Once in the air, the otter could not follow the cormorant.

The otter did not attempt pursuit. He was only intent on completing his swim to the other side of the estuary. As he swam on he noticed a small rocky islet which rose in front of him, and he headed straight for it, intending to rest for a few minutes. He ducked under the waves to approach it from under water. This enabled him to see any obstacles just below the surface which might otherwise catch him unawares. He walked up a ledge of rock under the water and poked his head out next to the granite islet. As he did so he saw a blur of movement in front of him, and a large dark shape slid from the rocks into the sea.

He turned his head to watch the spot where the shape had disapeared, and then saw a seal's head bob up between the waves. The seal studied him carefully for a full half minute, then swam back to the rocks, regaining its former position out on the kelp bed, which had been thrown down over the rock by the earlier receding tide. The seal proceeded to ignore the otter, who was unsure of how to react to this obviously large, but seemingly harmless creature which shared his amphibian habits.

He slid below the waves, and swam to a point close to the seal's position. As though echoing the seal's behaviour he too bobbed his head up between the waves, and studied the seal carefully. Then his curiosity got the better of him. He swam boldly towards her tail. The seal's head swung round to confront him and, unnerved, he shot back under water to surface once more right behind her tail, as though hoping to hide there while he considered his next move. She slewed round, twisting her head sideways till she could see him. Her eyes were aligned vertically now, as her head was completely turned on to one side. She watched him intently.

The otter gingerly ascended the kelp-covered rock. Pushing only his head forward, his body remained poised for flight, and his flaring nostrils inched towards the seal's tail. She immediately shifted her position indignantly to half-face him, slithering and scrabbling with one flipper on the kelp to steady herself.

The otter slowly retreated, a disappointed look on his face, as though he had hoped to nip her tail. He slowly backed into the waves and slid beneath them. He surfaced close to her head, his bright button eyes fixing on the seal. She grunted and blew out air, then flopped back to lie on the kelp bed and watched him carefully.

He swam up very slowly till he was a yard from her head. He stopped in the water, and gazed fixedly at her.

She stared back from above him with black eyes shrouded under deep brows. Her nostrils dilated as she whiffled her nose in slight rapid breaths, trying to catch the slightest trace of fear in

the otter's smell. There was none, so she slowly pushed her nose down the kelp towards him as he lay, stilled by fascination, in the sea. Their noses touched briefly, and then stayed close together for a few moments. The seal blinked, and slipping down past him she eased her way into the water beside him. He span away and dived, following her in a spiral down to the sea bed. A flick of her tail sent the seal pirouetting upwards, closely followed by the otter, which swam around her bulky body as they rose to the surface. There they swam around one another, playing in the waves. A game developed. First one would dash away, closely pursued by the other. Suddenly the tables were turned, and reversing direction the hunter became the hunted. The game was born out of a sense of fun shared by both mammals, and helped to relieve the boredom of their lone existence. It ended when the seal returned to the rocks for a final rest before sundown, and the start of her night's fishing.

The otter, realising the game was over, began the final short swim that brought him to the new land of his choice. His paws touched sand as he waded ashore. He paused in the breaking waves, and looked around for danger. Then, relaxing, he stepped out of the sea and ran up the open beach. Once he was amongst the rocks, he began to shake himself. Starting with his head he rotated the front half of his body in a clockwise direction. As soon as the movement commenced, it was echoed from the tail, but in the reverse direction. Water came whirling off each end of the otter's convulsing body, until the two opposing spray wheels met in a final flurry of fur around his ribs. He shook once more to rid himself of the excess water in his fur, and then rubbed himself dry, rolling on the shore and squeezing up against boulders to force the water out finally from his thick coat.

He looked about him once more, assessing his new environment, and made up his mind that a meal was necessary before departing into his new world.

Chapter Two

WHILE SEARCHING IN THE SURF FOR FISH, the otter kept an eye on the weather too. The sudden change to good weather that had coincided with his dream now seemed part of it.

While he crossed the estuary the gaping rent in the heavily clouded sky had moved on over the horizon. Gone too were the big white clouds and pale blue sky. Low grey cloud, fingering rain down to the sea now darkened the sky, turning the sea leaden. Squalls of sudden cold rain reached out towards him, and lashed on to the beach while he hunted. After one such squall the sky lightened a little, and the otter paused in his hunt as a shaft of light reached down through the clouds, catching his attention with its brilliance. It briefly threw a band of silver across the sea, and shafts of pale pearly light reached down to sparkle on the waves for a few brief seconds. Then it was gone, and the squalls returned to soak the otter as he turned over stones, and nosed into seaweed clumps looking for crabs. The wind swept the rain sideways, seeming to drive itself into his bones. The low cloud darkened the beach prematurely, blotting out the sun a half hour earlier than normal, and taking him into his first night in the new land.

His search for crabs took him to the weed beds lying among the rocks at the tideline. He pushed enquiring paws under the weed, his head arched back, and his hindquarters humped high as he scrabbled around in the weed searching for a movement from his intended prey. When he found a crab, he would whisk it out rapidly and spin it deftly to recapture it in such a way that its defensive claw was waving harmlessly away from his face. Then the otter bit into it, and made short work of its armoured body. He caught several crabs in this way, till his hunger was satisfied.

He went to a freshwater stream which spattered down over a low cliff at the far end of the beach. The continuously falling water had eroded a small basin where it struck the shore below. The otter lay in the bowl, turning his body this way and that, washing the salt out of his fur. He pushed his face up under the scattered falls of water. He bathed his salted eyelids, and then with open jaws darted back and forth to catch the erratic jets of water, gusted by the wind from side to side. Eventually the otter caught enough water to rinse out the salt from his gums and the soft skin which protected them.

The night gave him a sense of security, and he set off to explore the surrounding area. He began by making his way back to the other end of the beach. A buttress of rock thrust out across the beach on into the sea, marking the furthest end of the beach. It shone with damp black algae near the sea, rising into a band of green growths, till finally the rock itself emerged as red sandstone. The floor of the beach was islanded by large red boulders. Some of these were flecked with creamy deposits of quartz. Between the boulders coarse sand, sticky and dark gold, lay in large granular beds. The sand had been ground down over the millenia from the same stone as the boulders.

As he investigated the length of the beach the otter was searching for the scent of a spraint, indicating the presence of other otters. The beach bore no sign of any having passed by. He decided that he had the area to himself. He next spent several hours investigating the small stream that ran over the cliff. He followed it back to the peat bog at its source, and was unable to pick up any trace of an otter there either.

He noticed that there was an upturned boat at the rock-walled end of the beach. It rested on two baulks of wood, which raised it from the wet sand. Beneath the boat were stored a few lobster pot floats, and a large coil of rope. During his preliminary investigation of the beach the otter had noted the boat, and avoided it. Now he saw it was as unmoving as the rocks themselves, and could offer him a shelter for the night. He approached it warily to see if it was safe. He had never seen a boat like this before. Stopping every few paces, he circled it carefully. The boat was clinker-built of stout, well-varnished planks which overlapped one another and were rivetted to a wooden frame. It smelled of varnish and salt. There was a lingering scent of outboard motor fuel (oil and

9

petrol mixture) at the stern end. The rope coiled nearby was hairy, and smelled sweet and dry.

The otter came up to the transom of the dingy, and pushed his head beneath. Then he moved under the gunwhale and crawled right into the dry space inside. He touched the rope coil with his nose, and was tickled by coarse hairs. He snorted and then climbed up on to the coil, arranging his body in a curve that fitted it perfectly. His tail came right round to rest lightly over his nose. He dozed fitfully at first, woken frequently by the sudden pattering of heavy rain drops as they were flung at the boat by the rising wind. Eventually he became used to the sounds, and was lulled to sleep by the rhythmically repeated scrape and roar of waves first scouring the beach, then breaking back over it.

Just before daybreak he was woken by a new noise. It was the distant throb of an engine and seemed, as he listened, to be approaching him. He looked out from under the edge of the boat, and saw the tide was well out. It left a big space between his shelter and the water, and he could find no trace of movement in that direction. He moved to the other side of the boat and peered out. The noise was changing pitch now, dropping down, and rising again to a higher note. He was hearing for the first time the sounds of a Land Rover, dropping down through its gears as it met the stony track to the beach. The otter saw its lights beam out towards him, as it turned off the road to the track which led to the shore. He decided to stay hidden, and climbed back on to the rope coil. The throb of the engine echoed inside the boat making him uneasy. Then it suddenly stopped. He went to look out anxiously, and saw the lights pointing out along the beach. Then they were extinguished leaving a slight glow for a second. He heard a door shut with a smack, and the stones on the track scrunched together as a man began to walk towards the beach. The otter heard his steps all the way down the track till they crossed on to wet sand.

Still he kept hidden under the edge of the boat. While he was wondering which direction the footsteps had taken he was suddenly startled to see the shape of the man's head appear in silhouette against the moon in front of him. He wore a cap pulled down over his curly hair which escaped round his ears. The otter smelt his rubber boots now, and the tang of his heavy clothing. He could hear the rim of the rubber boots slap lightly against the man's trousers as he approached. The otter realised at last, with fear, that the man was coming straight to the boat. He withdrew his head, and raced out under the far side of the boat, across the empty beach, till he got to the big boulders.

The lobster fisherman caught a flash of movement out beyond his boat, then saw nothing more as the otter dodged behind the large stones. The otter heard the fisherman pause to look at him, and stayed hidden behind the boulders. Then he heard the man turn back to busy himself with his tasks. He listened to the dragging sound of the boat as it was rolled upright, and moved towards the sea, dodging from one boulder to the next, until he gained the cover of the waves. He swam along beside the beach till he reached its far end. He ran up under the rock buttress, and saw the man pulling a trailer under his boat, taking it to the sea. He turned to come along the back of the beach, then hesitated, fearing to go close to the Land Rover. Instead he climbed the rock buttress, and jumped down on to the adjoining beach. Halfway along it he found a drainage ditch leading inland under a hedge. The land sloped gently upwards across two fields to a farm, and the ditch led him towards the outbuildings. He turned left at the top of the field, following a second hedge by the edge of a ploughed field. The red soil was shining in the moonlight, moisture glistening on the smooth sides of the furrows. In the distance he saw the dark shape of mountains as the dawn began to lighten the sky beyond their rim.

His paws were becoming sticky with red soil, and he dived under the hedge into the adjoining field. A ditch ran on the far side, and he slipped into it to clean the clay off his feet. He was ascending the rising ground on grass once more, skirting the farm. He went through a hedge at the top of the field, and found himself on a road. He dashed over it and through the fence on its far side, to emerge on to rough moorland. As the grey light of dawn suffused the landscape he saw there was a small copse in front of him, which had been left by the farmer as cover for pheasants.

He made for it at once, running through wiry grasses and over soft quaking peat to reach it. As he ran looking for a place to lie up, he smelt the brackish odour of a pond. The heavy rich scent of decaying debris and black mud led him through the copse to its far side.

He saw a fallen tree by the water's edge. Its up-ended roots had been overgrown by brambles, and the space beneath offered a perfect hover for him, in which to pass the day. He looked for a way in, and found a rabbit run which penetrated its thorny fastness.

He slept lightly for some of the next six hours, waking at every new sound in the copse. The harsh calling of the pheasants woke him three times till he became used to them. A jay raised an alarm close to him, and twice he was roused by the thud of a rabbit stamping on the earth to warn others of his presence in his new hover.

When he finally awoke fully, it was early afternoon. He felt nervous and hungry. He lay absorbing the sounds and smells around him, checking that nothing dangerous was near. After a while he went out through the rabbit run to the pond. He slid quietly into it, and disappeared under the dark water. His bristly whiskers were tuned to the pressure waves in the water, and he sensed movement close by. He dived down, and pursued a bream that inhabited the pond. He caught it, and retreated into the hover to eat it. He feared going out near the farm in daylight, and decided to doze in the copse hover till dusk. He was extremely tired having slept so fitfully, and he did not have the confidence to explore the strange surroundings by day. He eventually fell to sleep, his head tucked into his haunches to shut out the light. Only his ears remained uncovered.

Chapter Three

IN THE LATE AFTERNOON the farmer who owned the copse returned, with his two dogs, from their visit to the distant market.

The dogs were cross-breeds. The larger of the two was a mixture of Border Collie and Alsatian, her black and white coat short-haired on a body too heavy for a Border Collie. The smaller dog was part Spaniel, mixed with Terrier. Both dogs were in the back of the Land Rover, and their claws clattered on the metal floor and tailgate as they scrambled out to land in the yard. They were delighted to be back, and dashed off in high spirits under the field gate adjoining the cowsheds, chasing each other over the farm lands. It was not until they reached the second field that they suddenly picked up the scent of the otter. They began to bark excitedly, and ran around in circles trying to determine where the scent came from. They soon set off towards the far hedge and ditch up which the otter had run the previous night. They followed his line towards the copse, noses down, and running with great concentration.

As he dozed, the otter heard the dogs barking, and was jerked into wakefulness. His head shot up as he listened closely to the sound, trying to tell whether it threatened him. It was coming from the ditch, and he realised they were on his scent, cutting him off from the sea.

He left the hover and plunged into the pond to reduce his smell. Then, emerging at the far side he ran out across the field, hidden from view by the copse. He ran parallel to the sea at first till he found a hedge leading back down to it. He shot under and ran behind it,

still hidden from the dogs. As he turned the corner he heard their clamorous barking reach a crescendo. They had found his strongly-scented resting place, and were looking for a way in. While they spent a few moments tunnelling down the rabbit run, the otter raced for the shore. He dropped down over a stone wall that separated the beach from the pastures. He could hear the thud of the bigger dog's feet on the hollow turf of the field as he set off across the beach. The dogs were on to him now, and had ceased barking. They ran hard, nose down, and were gaining on him. He glanced back as he neared the waves to see the pair come flying over the stone wall, their front paws lightly brushing it as they sped down towards him. Now they could see their quarry, and with frantic yelps of anticipation set off in pursuit. The otter reached the breaking waves with ten metres to spare, and rushed into them. He dived under the water and swam hard, away from the beach. Then he turned a right angle to follow the shore, keeping below the water till he was near the far end of the beach. Rising quietly under a mat of weed which floated by the rocky buttress, he peered back towards the shore.

The dogs dashed into the water after him. As the sea slowed their progress they began to bob about, turning their heads in each direction to try and catch sight or scent of the otter. They went back to the beach to re-establish the line, and ran around in confusion. The otter watched them from the weed bed, and then slipped under water to make his way around the end of the buttress. When he surfaced again he found that the land was rising steeply till it became a solid cliff. He swam off shore for half an hour, during which time there was no break in the high cliffs. At sunset a honking sound behind him made him pause. The calling ended in an echoing hollow cry of intense loneliness, and he then heard wingbeats coming towards him. He looked behind him and in the glowing sky he saw a large black bird. Its long pointed wings made a musical note that pulsed with the rhythm of each wingbeat. The bird uttered its lonely calls at intervals, flying in huge circles, as though it had lost its fellows. Its search took it over the cliffs eventually, and its sad cries faded away. The otter was growing tired and swam closer to the cliffs, looking for a break in the wall of rock. He found no break, but came up to a group of rocks that rose above the waves, and he wearily clambered on to them to rest. Dusk was falling, and he slept deeply for an hour. Then the rising tide broke over the rocks, sending spray high over him. It woke him instantly, and he looked out into the dark night. Wearily he climbed down the sheltered side of the dwindling island and resumed his swim.

He kept just off shore, always keeping the black mass of the cliffs that loomed against the night sky in sight. His progress was slow. He was moving mechanically now, forcing himself onwards to find a new home. He rested for a further two hours on a ledge of rocks at the base of the cliffs, and then caught a sole on the sea bed. He took it back to the rocks, and ate it fast. Once more he slipped into the sea and resumed his journey.

The dark line of the cliffs began to drop down to the sea as he looked ashore. He had swum through most of the night, with only three hours' rest, and was very anxious to stop. As he passed the low end of the cliffs he suddenly saw lights.

Opening up before him was a harbour, sheltering a few fishing boats. Their lights were ablaze as a group of men in yellow shiny oilskins began to unload the night's catch, taken at the height of the tide. Arc lamps on the jetty shone down on them as they loaded hoists with nets of glistening fish.

The otter hung in the water at the harbour's mouth, deterred by the clank of boots on metal decks and the whining motors of the hoists. He wanted to rest, to crawl out on to the hard ground and sleep. The wind brought the smell of diesel exhaust to his nose, its acrid fumes making his eyes smart. He could not stay. Wearily he turned away and swam past the harbour. The land rose up once more, but less steeply now. When he was out of sight of the sea wall he swam ashore and rested on a tumbled fall of rocks at the foot of a small cliff.

As the dawn light illuminated his surroundings he saw he was by a cave, and he slowly limped over to it. A brief inspection assured him it was free of occupants and he stiffly walked in. He slumped down on its dry floor, and fell instantly asleep. He lay in deep exhausted slumber until the low evening sun beamed briefly into the cave and woke him. He fished successfully, and set out once again to swim beside the rising cliffs. It was not long before they dropped away to sea level. Here the otter found a small bay at the mouth of a river, amid muddy salt flats. Where the land rose around it the mud took over completely, till the river was walled in by steep banks of dark and smelly mud.

As the otter passed between the mud banks he hoped to find an area where he could live for a while, perhaps even find a mate. He searched for fish, but to his surprise found none. He moved upriver through the cloudy water, relying on his vibrissae to sense the presence of fish. He received no signs of pressure waves. He noticed that the water had an odd taste to it. He surfaced on a bend in the river, and found to his discomfort that his head was surrounded by floating detritus. The backwash of the main stream had accumulated an assortment of plastic bottles and polystyrene pieces, which floated like ghosts on the scum in the dim light. Some greyish bubbles joined up in a spatter of still foam. The otter dived again, and decided to leave the area. It had been polluted, and was now a receptacle for the rubbish of the town further upstream. It held no fish. No birds visited it: it was a dead river.

Ahead of him the night sky was lit by a strange glow, as the lights of an industrial estate shone on plumes of smoke rising from high thin chimneys, which were carried across the estuary by off-shore breezes. Some of the smoke was yellow and thin, but most of it was heavy grey or white. The otter climbed the mud bank and ran towards the sea over sticky grasses. He crossed the mud flats, loath to enter the sea yet again. Just before the land rose once more he discovered a small river which ran at an angle to the cliffs, coming down through the higher land in a wooded valley.

He ran up beside the river into the wood with new hope. Once in the trees he dived into the river to rid himself of the odorous smell of mud flats which clung to his fur. Then he went upstream and caught a grayling.

Dawn found him travelling eagerly up the river two miles inland. Then as he rounded a bend he was abruptly faced with an end to his journey. There was an enormous curved wall rising in front of him. At its base the river spewed out through a sluice gate. The sides of the wall stretched away into the trees on either side, and its top rose high, so he had to crane his neck to see it. He was blocked by a dam which held back a reservoir in the now flooded valley, previously drained by the river alone.

The otter turned back to the wood, and found a fallen tree under which to pass the day in sleep. At dusk he caught two fish in the space of an hour, and then resumed his journey back to the sea. That night he followed the beaches that lay beneath the cliffs for four hours, until the incoming tide forced him to swim again. The cliffs were unbroken, and dawn found him searching for a hover in which to rest. Eventually he found a cave at the foot of the cliffs, and he went in to sleep, up on a ledge clear of the high tide line. When he awoke, he lay still for some time, as he resigned himself to the knowledge that he must move on once more. Eventually he roused himself and entered the water. He swam out below the towering cliffs, and wearily headed west. The dark outline of the cliffs changed as the night wore on, and he noticed that mountains could be seen rising behind them in places.

In the early hours of the morning the retreating tide allowed him to return to the exposed beach and travel close under the cliffs on stretches of sand between rocky outcrops. Shoulders of rock reached out from the cliffs in places to force him temporarily into the sea as he rounded them, but mostly the beach highway was smooth, and he travelled fast. As he swam round one of the arms of rock in the pre-dawn glimmer of first light, his senses quickened. The cliffs fell back to form a small bay. Their sides were thickly covered with hazel bushes. The floor of the valley between the slopes was composed of rocky outcrops enclosing gentle inclines of grass. Down the centre of the valley ran a small stream. The jumbled rocks near the beach provided a secure hover for the otter, who at last experienced a sense of relief. He was too tired to explore the valley, but he felt in his bones that it was a good place. He went to the stream to wash off the salt which impregnated his fur, and to drink the sweet cool water which came down from the hill. As he looked up the valley he could see a single mountain, smoothly rounded, which rose up behind the highest rocks of glowing purple in the dawn. Its summit was encircled in wispy patches of cloud which wreathed their vapours around it as they spilled down.

The otter turned away, and clambered up the rocks into an opening amongst them. He lay, relaxed at last, and looked out at the sea in which he had spent so much time travelling. He closed his eyes, and decided that he would explore the valley when he woke. He felt that he had arrived at an area in which he could establish a range of his own. It did not occur to him then that other otters might have found it too, and that a mature dog otter was in residence in the next bay.

19

THE YOUNG OTTER WOKE in mid-afternoon. He fished successfully in the bay, and set out to explore his valley. It was quite small, and as he climbed one side of the enclosing slopes, he found it led down again into a second larger bay. He lay on top of the ridge, and gazed about him. He could see more mountains now, stretching back from the bay. At the foot of the mountains the land was sparsely wooded, and held a number of small farms. Streams from the hills converged on the bay, and disappeared into the shingle and sand of its beaches. Offshore there were three rocky islets, which even at low tide were always surrounded by water. Out on the islands black shags stood silhouetted against the sparkling sea, drying their wings in the afternoon sun. The hard rocks were covered at their lowers levels with kelp, on which lay a small colony of grey seals. They blended with the background so well that at first they were hardly discernible. However they shifted their bulky bodies occasionally, so the otter noticed their movement. The seals had chosen one particular islet as their resting place. It rose well clear of the sea at one end, while sloping low to the water at the other. By high tide it would be almost completely awash, but the tide was only flooding as the otter gazed out. He moved down to the beach below and caught a crab. Then he retreated to a high rocky ledge to eat it. He remained there watching the sand and islets before him.

The seals were in two groups. The cow seals lay high on the rising end of the islet, leaving the calves, some still in their white baby fur, to occupy the lower, kelp-strewn rocks. A roman-nosed bull seal was near the rocks, waiting to rejoin his harem. His head sank out of sight, then suddenly a few metres away the whole seal leapt full out of the waves, with arching back. As it crashed down on the water it sent a shower of spray into the air, and the otter heard the smack of its impact on the waves.

The incoming tide spilled into hollows scooped into the gradual rise of the beach, lifting bladder wrack pods that fringed the rocks. The water gurgled as it surreptitiously laid its sly embrace around them. Stealthily its imperceptible progress changed the shape of the sand bars and pools on the sand. Eventually the rising water reached the lowest of the basking seals, running a cold finger round their bellies as it eased up through the kelp.

The youngsters shrank from the water, raising their heads and tails, and lifting flippers high to avoid its cold embrace. They teetered, balancing on their flanks, as the buoyant water lifted them from their couch of kelp and threatened to scoop them off the rocks. Anxious craning heads, counterbalanced tails were held high as they swayed precariously on the ocean's swell.

The seals were determined to remain sunning themselves for as long as possible, but finally the water lifted them clear of the kelp. Then, with resignation, they pushed their heads down and glided under the waves. Each seal repeated this elaborate act of evasion as the islet was engulfed by the tide, till none were left on the rocks.

Below the otter's high ledge, the arm of the bay terminated in a mass of rock that rose against the sea at the end of a sand bar. In the shadow of the dark granite stood a heron, stock still. It blended with the grey-green rock and weed. Water was lapping at either side of the sand bar, ambushing a narrow curving land bridge to the rock. The sand turned dark, and then disappeared under the creeping tide. Determinedly the heron stood its ground, gazing down into the shallow water that covered its feet now. Soon its long legs were half-immersed in the swirling tide, but it remained totally unmoving. The bird held its ground for a further ten minutes, till a slopping wavelet raced round the rock to slap up its rear quarters. With a shriek of disgust it shook itself violently and flew away, croaking a low grumbling protest at such an affront to its dignity.

Shags, which had left the seal rock with the rising tide, now began returning to it to preen and dry their out-hung wings. Then they rested for a short while before flying straight and low over the waves once more. The tide was running in fast now, creating a race between the islets and the

shore. The shags flew out to the start of the tide-race, and settled on the swiftly moving water, facing upstream. In this position they were carried rapidly backwards while they gazed intently into the waves looking for a glint of reflected light from silvery scales. When they glimpsed a shimmering fish they dived to pursue it under the racing water.

When the current had carried them back past the islands, they rose up and took flight till they reached its head again, and repeated the search.

Further along the bay, as the tide moved in, a variety of wading birds were being hustled before it. Oyster catchers, bright orange bills and white flashes catching the light, piped noisily across the shore. Sometimes half a dozen of their number made short low flights to new ground, determined to investigate it before the lapping waves spilled across it. Dunlin moved in short erratic runs, while Turnstones busied themselves at their task.

At first the otter did not notice the curlews among the beach boulders. Their softly mottled brown-and-cream plumage blended perfectly with the stones on the strand. Their presence was revealed when they turned towards the land to show fleetingly their white breast feathers. One of them called, a rising warbled note, and suddenly they all took flight together. Of the twenty or so that rose into the air, only three had been noticed by the otter.

Out on the waves a pair of Red-Throated Divers elegantly smoothed their way over the waves. They were svelte and assured. By contrast a ruffianly flock of gulls were standing on a spit of sand awash with besieging salt water. For once they were silent as they fed with total concentration, moving back every few minutes to keep pace with the tide. Out amongst the floating strands of kelp was a pair of Red-Breasted Mergansers. Their subtle brown colouring mingled with the background of sea and kelp in perfect harmony. Only the irridescent bottle-green head of the drake drew attention to them. All the birds were feeding with great eagerness, before the relentless tide covered the rocks and sand. The distribution of the flocks changed slowly as the tide re-arranged their feeding positions.

As the sea flooded in, so the sun sank towards it. The sky was banded with long narrow banks of grey cloud. The fiery red ball emerged below the lowest band, and briefly threw a last sliver of light out over the grey sea, turning the waves silver and their foaming tops pink as it caught the wave tops in its glow. This moment was short-lived as the sucking sea drew the rim of the sun down into its depths. It swallowed the dark pink ball of fire, the sea glowing coppery red, and showing frothy pink wave tops for an instant where they shattered on the beach. Then the sun was drowned, and its sudden quenching prompted a last defiant burst of song from the wrens in the hazel bushes behind the otter.

A cold wind came into the bay, ruffling the steely surface of the water, and sending a shiver down the otter's haunches. He moved down to the water intent on fishing, and worked his way around the rocks into his small haven of a bay.

As he departed the icy wind sent a shuddering gust over the big beach. It was as though its ice-breath was herald to the night, and on to the newly cold beach walked the dim grey shape of a large dog otter. He came across the tumbled rocks at the far end, which had hidden him at first. His sepia coat blended in the dark with shadowy stones and kelp. It was only as he stepped on to the dwindling sands that his shape became discernible. He moved boldly across the few metres of remaining sandspit, sending the gulls into raucous indignant flight as he appeared amongst them. He ran into the sea and hunted the bottom for flounders. As he passed close to the rocks a stirring on the sea bed betrayed the presence of a large sole. Turning aside he sped to scoop it off the sand before it could flee. He rose to the surface with it in his jaws, and swam back to the shore. There he climbed on to a rock to eat the struggling fish. A few bites left it limp under his paws, and he tore into it with great relish. He returned to the sea, and hung floating under the waves, letting the sucking tide draw him back and forth above the beach, as he watched for movement in the sand. Eventually he spotted another flounder, and he caught it in his paws, transferring it swiftly to his jaws. He lay on his back in the shallow water and tucked into the fish. The restless waves carried him towards the beach, bumping him on the sand as they drew him back and forth. Discarding the half-eaten fish he righted himself, and walked out of the surf to the turf at the top of the beach. There he rubbed his jaws along the short springy grass, cleaning off the remaining fish scales and remnants of flesh.

He went to drink from one of the small streams that ran out on to the beach. He followed the stream up its boggy course till it deepened by a shoulder of rock. Here he was able to immerse his body by the rock, and wash the salt out of his fur. He rolled on a clump of spiky golden grasses to dry himself. Then he glimbed the rock above the stream and curled up on the springy lichens that grew over it. He lay facing the beach. The rising ground behind him faded into a jumble of dark tones.

While the big dog otter was dozing above the bay, the young otter was fishing in the adjoining one. His pursuit of a shoal of mackerel led him back into the big bay around the arm of rocks. He failed to catch the fleet fish, so decided instead to search the high rock pools for crabs. He soon found one, and took it, up to the rocks above to eat it. The report as he cracked open its shell reached the ears of the dozing big dog otter by the stream. He recognised the sound of another otter eating, and thinking it might be his mate he called, a high short whistle. The young otter heard it and, answering it at once, began to run up the beach towards the stream.

The big dog came down from his couch to meet him. They caught sight of each other at a distance of about ten metres. When the young otter saw the size of the stranger he stopped in his tracks. The big animal kept on coming, arriving at a trot to stop right in front of the youngster. He shrank back in fear, as though he would like to disappear into the sand. He stood trembling as the big male smelt his hind quarters, and then huffed his disapproval of the newcomer.

This was too much for the younger otter who turned tail and fled towards the sea. The challenger followed him closely, whickering his displeasure at finding an intruder on the edge of his range, and enforcing it with brisk nips on the rear of the retreating youngster. His tail and rump were bitten several times before he shot under the waves, and torpedoed out to sea. Having driven off his rival so successfully the bigger otter did not pursue him further, but was content to watch as the youngster's head appeared heading round the arm of rocks and out of the bay, amongst moonlit waves.

Chapter Five

THE YOUNG OTTER returned to the small bay, and painfully made his way up the beach to the stream. He immersed his stinging rump and tail in the cool water, and gradually lowered his whole body to lie on the marble bed of the stream. He ducked his eyes under the flowing fresh water, soothing his salt-caked lids. Gradually the stream eased the hot pain, and he moved on to the grass to lick his wounds.

Hunger drove him to seek crabs under the wrack beds of the beach. He ate two, and then after cleaning himself, made his sorrowful way up the valley to find a secure hover in which to lie up. Among the tumbled rocks of the hillside he found a series of fallen boulders that had been laid over one another by a long departed glacier. Spaces between the boulders were investigated in turn by the otter, who chose a long narrow passage in their midst and curled up at its far end. He slept for an hour, and awoke in the early night, hungry and sore. He hesitated to go into the sea, and managed by good fortune to surprise a young rabbit as it fed outside the rocks. He returned to creep in amongst the boulders and slept restlessly through the night until early morning.

The dawn woke him, and he ventured out once more to stretch his limbs and lick his smarting wounds. He gathered bracken in his jaws and pushed it back into the rocky hole. Then he climbed in and rearranged it into a bed. He slept throughout the daylight hours, undisturbed by the big dog otter, who was at the edge of his range – and had now returned to his mate further inland.

When the otter awoke it was already growing dark, and he went

out into the valley to explore it thoroughly. He moved less painfully now. His wounds were responding to the careful attention he gave them with his healing tongue. The bay faced south-east and was sheltered by arms of rock that ran to the sea on either side. On one side the rocks were formed from the molten lava of a long dead volcano. The lava had been full of steam bubbles when as a red liquid it flowed from the mountain. The seething mass had been instantly solidified where it ran into the sea, trapping huge air bubbles up to thirty centimetres in diameter. Over the centuries erosion had weathered the rock so that it now presented sharp and rough textured craters on its surface. It was impossible to walk over it without suffering lacerations from its needle-like surface. The other arm of rock which separated the bay from the range of the big otter was shaped like a wall, rising sheer from the sea. It changed texture as it ascended in layered strata, to a height of thirty metres. The beach sloped up a valley to the foothills of the big mountains. It was sheltered from the wet south-westerly winds that had been bringing rain ever since the otter crossed to the new land.

The valley was populated by a horde of rabbits. These in turn attracted buzzards and a stoat. Kestrels, too, regularly patrolled the hillside. Cattle were grazed at the head of the valley – black, fierce-looking and independent beasts, who were left to roam free. When they came across the otter loping up their pasture they crowded round it inquisitively, reaching down suspicious pink nostrils to gasp and snuffle at the small brown creature newly arrived in their midst. The otter stood his ground for a few moments and suddenly, overwhelmed by their black overbearing heads, he withdrew into the bracken and fled. He had been born and reared on watermeadows, in a flat landscape, and was overawed by the fierce cattle, stern mountains and harsh rocky coast line, so different from the lush and gentle environment of the Levels he grew up amongst. His sense of loss returned to swamp his senses.

He still found movement painful when he stretched his hind limbs, and experienced a greater awareness of the pain as his loneliness returned. He suddenly felt enormously tired, and wandered slowly down by the stream to leave it for his hover in the rocks.

For four days he stayed in the valley, resting and recovering. On the fourth afternoon the wind changed, swinging right round the bay to the east. A storm was rising out at sea. The valley, instead of affording shelter, was now directly exposed to the gale force east wind. It brought ice on its breath, and dashed salt spray into the shore to silver the grass. It funnelled up the valley, shrieking its way in amongst the boulders that enclosed the otter. He huddled into the rocks, turning his back on the fierce wind, and sinking his nose into his tail. The storm tore its relentless way into every crevice, shaking the valley trees with its furious blasts. Their branches rattled together or creaked where they crossed one another. The otter did not hunt that night, but lay huddled and shivering as the wind tried to pluck him from his shelter.

Towards dawn the storm abated a little, and allowed the otter a chance to search for food. The sea was too rough to risk a swim by the rocks, so he searched for food under the banks of weed at the edge of the beach instead. He decided while eating that he must get out of the valley and find shelter from the raging wind. Since he could not go by sea, he determined to leave by the valley. After his meal he set off up the hillside, his fur blown backwards at times by the force of the elements. His ears hurt with the cold moaning wind, which reached a crescendo as he neared the top of the ridge flanking the upper end of the valley. He found his way barred by a stone wall, which he ran over, and continuing uphill in its lee. He found protection behind the ancient stones. Then, as the hill carried on over and down again towards the sea, he was forced to turn inland once more. He crossed an area of bracken and rock, still climbing. Across the top of the rocks ran a second wall. Just as he topped the wall, he saw a man coming towards him with a lantern. The man's shining clothing flopped wildly in the wind. At once the otter jumped round, and shot back behind the wall. He dashed into the bracken, and hid. The man came up to the wall, having glimpsed the otter, and swung his lantern over it. He saw no sign of the creature, and went on his way to check on the cattle.

The otter watched him go from deep in the bracken. When the swinging lantern had

28

disappeared he came out of hiding, and hurried across the rocks below the crest of the hill, and into a meadow. At the top of the meadow was a derelict stone byre. The walls had fallen in, forming piles of moss-covered stone on the old floor. Nettles had grown up between the stones. The otter crept into the byre, and found a hollow deep in the rockpile, where he sheltered from the fierce wind. Somewhere nearby the wind rattled a sheet of corrugated iron at intervals, and moaned its way around the corners of the stone shed beneath the tin roof.

Beyond the shed was a large caravan, sheltered between the shed, and an empty house below it. The wind was rising in strength and by midnight it had reached storm force. As it swung north of east a supremely savage gust tore between the stone shed and the solid house, impacting on the caravan like a ram. The van crashed on to its side, slid down the slope, and then was rolled on its roof by the urging gale. It toppled once more and began to disintegrate as the wind entered the broken windows and unhinged door, and blew apart the panels that had formed its walls. They sailed through the night to land up to two hundred metres from the house, and were scattered down the slope below the shed.

The first crash woke the otter, who crouched shivering with terror at the subsequent cacophony of the rolling caravan. He stayed put, not willing to face the terrors of the storm, and eventually fell into a weary sleep.

He awoke, disorientated, to find it was broad daylight and that quiet had come to the hill. The roaring wind had blown itself out. He lay in a stupor for a few minutes, blinking at the bright sunlight outside the stone pile. He adjusted his body and relaxed, at peace with the day. He fell into easier deeper sleep now, and did not wake until late in the afternoon.

Outside the byre the wreckage of the caravan lay strewn across the landscape. Pink pads of insulation had been scattered among the bushes and into the bottom of the byre. Slices of board, damp and broken into jagged pieces, lay all around the meadow. The big ash tree that grew by the barn had lost a branch, which now lay in the grass at the tree's roots.

The otter moved away from the storm-wracked area and back into the valley, which seemed welcoming by comparison. As he looked over the ridge into it, he saw bright sea and blue sky ahead of him. The late afternoon sun warmed his fur, and he hurried down to the shore to seek a meal. He had not eaten the previous night, and was now very hungry. He caught a large flounder, and demolished it quickly. Then he went to lie out on the warm rocks by his hover. As he was

29

dozing he was startled awake by the sound of voices. A couple were picking their way down the valley towards the beach, and had a dog with them.

The otter half-rose to slide round into the cavern amongst the rocks, and turned round at its end to lie facing the hover entrance, some three metres deep inside it.

Meanwhile the couple walked down by the stream talking together. Their dog, a black labrador bitch, was trotting at their heels when she caught a slight scent of the otter. She stopped, and lifted her head testing the breeze for further clues. Then she set off at a trot moving away from the stream towards the rocks where the otter lay.

The couple were deep in conversation, and did not hear the dog's feet change direction on the grass. Her black nose drew her straight towards the hover, and she grew excited at the strength of the scent. She began to whine and bark in a mixture of urging sound, that brought the couple out of their conversation to stand still and call her. The dog ignored their shouts and began to scrabble at the stone entrance which was too small to give her access. The unyielding rocks forced her to cease her efforts, and she pushed her nose into the entrance as far as possible.

The otter had remained still throughout, hoping to go unnoticed, but at the sight of the dog's head filling the entrance he reacted savagely. He began to produce sounds somewhere between a scream and a snarl which pulsed out towards the labrador with terrifying malevolence. The otter's whickering rose in intensity as the note changed to a pure scream, and he prepared to charge the dog. The labrador shot back out of the entrance at the sound, just avoiding the otter who rushed past her in a mixture of fear and aggression.

The couple, who heard the otter's savage cries came running up, concerned for the dog's safety. They saw a flash of brown as the otter disappeared into the hazel bushes. A few seconds later they saw their labrador, who fled back towards them with her tail between her legs. She arrived quivering, and sat pushed against their legs. They shouted sharply at her for not returning when called, then spoke more softly as they realised how frightened she really was. They bent down and smoothed her ruffled fur, stroking and calming her, and went down to the beach, where they engrossed her in fetching sticks from the waves.

Chapter Six

THE OTTER COULD NOT STAY in the valley with the dog about. He watched the couple take her down to the beach, and then set off up the valley, following the stream back to the peatbog in which it rose. From there he climbed out of the valley. He ran up the ridge in the fading afternoon light, and followed it behind three cottages. A track led towards the mountain, edged with marshy ground and growing beds of yellow iris. The tall yellowing leaves still offered good cover, and he ran parallel to the track through the tall irises. He crossed a wood, and ran uphill over moorland which led up to the big mountain. Then, seeing nothing but open ground ahead, he dropped towards the sea once more. Crossing the slope he met a small stream, and turned to go up it around the flank of the mountain.

The stream led up through peat beds to a point where the ground levelled out in a cwm below the final steep hump of the mountain, which rose darkly above him. The stream's source was a small lake in the cwm. As the otter climbed beside the stream, he topped the last rise and saw the lake ahead of him. It lay in a slight depression below him. At its far end grew a few stunted rowan trees, by large slabs of rock. The lake was filled with reeds. An old wooden jetty stood rotting near the stream, and a boat was tied to a metal stake, driven into the peat nearby.

At the junction of lake and stream the otter paused and looked around him. The bowl of the cwm was undulating, covered in a mixture of grasses, kept short by rabbits. Heather grew in patches by the stonier edge of the bowl, and led up to the steep slope of the mountain itself.

Beside the lake rabbits had tunnelled warrens into the undulating ground, and the otter went to investigate one of these. It was an old warren, the holes worn large by long use, and it had been deserted by the rabbits long since. The otter chose the largest hole, and proceeded to open it up further, as a temporary shelter. Finding the earth was soft and sandy, he dug back quickly, showering out earth with his forepaws, shooting it between his wide-spread rear legs, and holding his rudder out to one side. Within ten minutes he had disappeared into the warren, which expanded inside to afford him a chamber in which he could lie down. Not content, he enlarged that as well to give himself space to turn. Then he went out to the lake and cleaned himself with a swim.

Night had fallen during his arrival at the lake, and now he went fishing. He caught three trout, and ate them one by one on the grass by the jetty. He must have been thinking about the holt in the warren as he fished, because he returned to it and dug a second entrance inwards through a connecting hole to the chamber. This gave him a second escape route, which emerged behind the bank beyond the hump housing the warren. The otter went to the edge of the cwm to collect heather, which he carried in his jaws to make a bed. He placed the woody material on the sand, covering it with softer bunches of grasses. This gave him an area of sieve-like bedding which allowed the water to drain from his coat, and enabled the top of the bed to dry again quickly. He had learned to make a bed that way from watching his mother do it for the family while he grew up. She had, by example, also taught him the wisdom of having more than one exit from a holt. He had not dug a holt of his own before. Being on the move continually he had contented himself with temporary hovers. Now, with the lake apparently free of other otters and hidden high in the hills, he felt that he could stay, and so went to the trouble of making a home. The need for a second exit was reinforced in his mind by his recent experience with the dog. He had been lucky that it was a gentle labrador that had found him, and not an aggressive terrier.

He came out of the holt covered in sand once more, and ran to the lake under the night sky, in order to wash his fur clean. Above him glinted bright stars, peeping through big clouds which marched across the heavens. Strong winds pushed the clouds steadily along, but down in the cwm the breeze was light, fended off by the bulk of the mountain. He found an eel in the muddy bottom of the lake and caught it. He ate it on the shore, and then ran along the edge of the lake to explore his new domain.

He travelled around the curving shore, smelling each little beach, and investigating the mossy tussocks that rose at its edge. He found no trace of other otters, and grew more confident as he progressed. At the far side of the lake by the rowans he placed a spraint on the rocks at the water's edge, and carried on round towards his holt. As he came down the last unexplored part of the shore, he heard a movement on the side of the mountain. He froze, and shrank to the ground. As he listened he heard the muffled clatter of hooves on rock. Then he heard a bleating sound, and a deeper response, as three sheep loomed out of the darkness towards him. He rose, unconcerned, and completed the circuit of the lake shore back to his holt. He lay in the chamber, on his dry bed, and closed his eyes. He was contented at last – no longer forced to move on, this was a range he felt he could occupy.

The next night, having slept long and well, he explored the area around the lake leading up into the mountain. He discovered small hollows in the cwm filled with wet springy moss-covered bogs, which gave nourishment to low-growing birch trees. They ducked under the wind as they leaned away from it in the dipping ground. He surprised a grouse which flew off low and weaving, stuttering abuse at him.

He had arrived in the valley on a Tuesday. This implied nothing to him, but it meant he had moved in just after a fishing party had left it on the previous Sunday.

For four days he had the lake area to himself, but on the fifth, Saturday, his idyll was destroyed. At around nine o'clock in the morning, while he was deep in his first sleep, a party of anglers arrived at the jetty. They came up quietly, and were beginning to take their chosen positions by the water, when one of them noticed an otter paw mark in the mud at its edge.

He called over one of his companions, to verify his discovery, and both men agreed that it was indeed an otter's paw print. They walked together around the lake a little, and found four spraints on an old stump by the water. This convinced them that the otter was still probably at the lake. They began to wonder where it had its holt, since the cover was sparse in the cwm. They walked towards the end of the lake, and searched the outcrops where the rowans gripped the rocks with finger-like roots. They could find no trace of an opening for a holt, and continued round till they came to the rabbit warren.

The freshly dug earth outside a larger than normal hole convinced them they had found the holt. A run in the grass led straight to the lake, and clinched the certainty in their minds. They had approached quietly, and now signalled to each other, not speaking. They both approached the holt cautiously. Soon they could smell the otter's fishy, musky scent. Wondering how many of their valued trout it had taken from the lake, they determined to drive it away. One of the men signalled to the other to watch the holt, while he went back to his three companions. He approached them with his hand to his mouth, preventing them from calling a greeting as he arrived. He told them, in low tones, of his certainty that there was an otter in the rabbit warren beyond the iron post.

The men gathered their knives, and their long fishing umbrellas, which they kept furled. They approached the holt watcher quietly and whispered instructions to each other. Two of the group moved quietly round the mound, and found the otter's escape hole. They positioned themselves on the soft turf close by and knelt, watching carefully.

The man who had originally been left to guard the holt came softly round to check that his companions were in position. He returned to the others and nodded. The men suddenly began to shout, and rattle stones in a tin while the leader took his long umbrella, and poked it inquisitively down the enlarged rabbit hole.

The otter woke suddenly, and lay cowering, ears flat on his head and eyes staring, at the unexpected tumult outside. He saw the umbrella poking across the tunnel in front of him, unable to negotiate the bend in the hole. He spat and huffed at it, and then turned to race out of the escape hole.

He burst from the hole and dived, whickering furiously, at the two kneeling men, who fell sideways to give him passage and disappeared into the heather. They followed his progress by

watching the waving bushes, till he reappeared by the lake. He ran to the far end, and they lost sight of him on the mountainside. That was the last they saw of him.

The men walked back to the lake, wondering at the otter's ferocity, and grumbling that it had probably cleaned the lake of trout. They set up once more, and began to fish.

Chapter Seven

THE OTTER WAS NOW FORCED TO FLEE the cwm in broad daylight, and run out over its edge back down the hill below. He could see the shining sea beyond the long slow descent ahead of him, and headed for it. The wind carried the rich aroma of seaweed and salt up the hillside, tempting him to return to the escape route of the shores once more. He swung to his right where the hill wore a mantle of dark golden bracken. Once under the canopy of dry tendrils he could move unseen. He slowed to a trot, and worked his way down through the cover till he came to a fence. Beyond the fence lay farmland with its inherent danger, so he kept under cover and turned along the fence, to drop slightly down at an angle which took him around the edge of the fields. Bordering the farm was a plantation of young conifers. He slipped into the trees and began to search for a hiding place. He burrowed his way into a knot of cut pine branches and lay under the pile on the dark dry earth. He napped the day away, before rising to continue his journey back to the sea in the late afternoon.

He came out of the wood on a track which had been trodden by sheep, and led to the high land bordering the sea. The ground fell steeply away on his right to a deserted house on the shore. To the left it dropped into a shallow valley, by which it descended to the sea. At the head of the valley was a meadow, and at its base, separating it from the wild land below, was a dry stone wall.

The otter moved down through the tall wild flower stems and thistles of the meadow, and ran up over the wall. A flock of bramblings were busy feeding on the last of the autumn crop of thistle down. As the otter came over the wall he surprised the flock, which rose into the air as one, and twittered angrily above him. The birds refused to move far, and he ran on through a cloud of beating wings. They fluttered back to the ground behind him, and continued feeding as though nothing had happened.

He worked his way down the shallow valley towards the shore. Where the grassy floor of the valley met the beach it was eaten into by the tides, forming a maze of small black channels which penetrated the turf, creating small isolated humps of green. The otter made his way through the dark water on to the shingle beach. He ran down the beach, out of the exposed valley and along under the steep slopes to the west. He followed the coast for a couple of hours searching, as always, for a territory that was safe to live in and had food available.

His quest for a new home had now taken him on a journey that had lasted for three weeks. He began to feel that he was doomed to a life of continuous searching, both for a territory and a companion in his wanderings. It was a depressed otter who moved ever westwards under the steeply angled land. The night grew colder and seemed endless as he humped over sand and shingle. He was forced to turn inland occasionally by precipitous rock faces, or to swim round them. His paws were sore from the rough texture of the rocks. He often had to climb only to drop into yet another beach. It was in this state of numb resignation and weariness that he noticed a new sound in the distance. It was a roaring that rumbled a lower note than the scrape of wave-shifted shingle and came from beyond the lowering cliffs, where they jinked in craggy confusion down to the shore ahead. The otter moved forward till he was by the rockfalls that marked the meeting of sea and cliff. As he clawed his way over the jumble of boulders he heard the noise grow in intensity until, as he stared towards its source, it filled his senses with its powerful sound.

Beyond the rockfall opened a small bay, at whose back a river tumbled down on to the shore from low cliffs. It dropped first to a ledge, then fell in one big jet on to the stones of the beach. The fall was about ten metres wide, and carried a huge volume of water. The otter could see no way of climbing the precipitous waters with their weighty mass foaming at the base of the cliff. He ran up the rockfall and moved to the cliffs around the bay. It did not take him long to arrive at the side of the river where it ran towards the falls. He journeyed up it, descending into a rocky gorge as he did so. The river had cut its way deeply into a rock fault, and now ran well below the

land. It boiled through the gorge, in a spate swollen by the recent rains which had raised the water table in the mountains.

The otter went up the gorge, past swishing pools and foaming races, where the river was constricted by the rock walls, and forced to find passage over rocky ledges. He spent some of the journey in the river, staying close to the gorge walls, where the current ran more gently. Gradually the gorge widened, and the river abated its fury. The water grew shallower as the river widened, and the otter was able to climb out on to the land at the top. He found himself at the side of a huge valley which bent away into the distance and was hemmed in by mountains on either side. They loomed high and dark against the night sky. Pine trees grew at intervals along the river, finding roothold in the rocks that enclosed the waters. The valley was much larger than the others he had experienced, and seemed to sweep away for ever in a long curve.

As he continued upstream, he wondered if there were any other otters in the area. After a mile he found his first clue – a spraint placed on a boulder above the river. The scent was not very old, perhaps two days at most. Once again he felt his senses quicken as he anticipated meeting another otter.

He ran up beside the gorge, passing through a small wood, and there he found a second spraint. This was very fresh, and he thought he must be near the other otter. He stood up, and threw a penetrating whistled call upriver. He paused before dropping down, to listen for an answer. None came, so he ran forward to hurry upstream. Half a mile's travelling brought him to a very fresh spraint, and the remains of a fish by the river bank. He stopped to investigate the spraint, and then stood up to call again. As he listened for an answer he heard a faint reply ahead of him. He ran on, calling at short intervals. The replies became louder as the two otters moved swiftly towards each other. Now he saw movement ahead of him, and in a few moments the two creatures met. They went slowly up to each other, and stood head to head as they exchanged scents. Then they moved head to tail to each establish which sex the other was.

They were both young males, and from the friendly disposition of the new otter, the youngster quickly understood that he was not paired with a bitch, but roamed the area in isolation. The new dog otter was in fact some six months older than the incomer, and had left his family to find companionship and a home range. He had come over the mountains following hill streams till eventually settling in the valley, which was about seven miles long. Five hill farms occupied the valley, running sheep on its floor and the lower flanks of the hills. It held a wide variety of habitats for the dog otter, being wooded in places, and having a lake at its higher end.

The otters spent the last few hours into the dawn travelling up the river towards the head of the valley. In the wintry dawn they moved into a holt just near the lake. From behind its entrance they looked out into the jagged black mountains that encircled the valley head beyond the far bank of the river.

They spent the next three nights exploring the range together. The resident dog otter knew exactly where to fish in the quieter stretches of the river. He had established five holts down the length of the river, the last being a mile upstream of the falls. Streams ran down from the mountains, and the otters travelled up them into bogland as they investigated everything together. They avoided the farms where sheepdogs were ever watchful and barked if they smelt an otter on the wind. The weather brightened for a few days in early November, and the young otter decided to revisit the shore. He led the elder dog back past the edge of his range, down through the gorge towards the sea. The passage was easier now, as the river had returned to its usual winter level and ran quietly down its rocky road to the sea, until it came to the cliff-falls where it thundered loudly on to the beach boulders. He introduced his new companion to his favourite stretches of sea fishing, and rock-pool hunting. The otters were both uplifted by each other's company and found a new zest in life. They began to spend a great deal of time playing together after eating. Whichever one finished eating first would keep his distance from the other. The instant the last to finish had gulped down his meal, the first would huff impatiently at him. Often the second otter would take no notice, and turn his back to groom himself. That was a signal to the impatient partner to whicker a warning as he dived towards the tail of his companion. All thought of

grooming vanished as the second otter shot a glance backwards, to see open jaws advancing at full speed towards his tail. He shot forward and twisted his tail sideways, drawing it clear of the closing teeth intent on nipping it. The two otters then careered over the beach in hot pursuit of each other. One would dodge behind a rock, only to jump round and leap out as the other came past – reversing the chase. Then the leading otter would suddenly throw out his feet, braking to a stop and flip over on to his back, thrusting up with all four feet as he did so. The advancing otter was usually gathered on the rising paws, and bowled off course. Quick as lightning, the rolling otter would scramble on to the sprawling form, and deliver a quick nip before jumping clear to career away behind the boulders, and so the game would continue.

Sometimes they played vertical games, which began underwater, ascended through its surface up the banks of the river, and even up over low branches of trees. Every game was different in detail, but showed the same basic tactics of surprise – run, ambush, a quick nip, and run on again. Sometimes, when they played this furious tag on the river bank they left large areas of muddy tracks and flattened grasses, which showed where they had charged through the wet landscape. They had learned their games from their mothers, sisters and brothers, as a skill to be used – in fighting if necessary, but the nips in play were always teasing, never vicious, and intended to note a point scored, rather than inflict a wound.

After playing, the young otters would relax side by side, wedged against one another to gain maximum comfort as they lay exhausted by their frantic chase. They groomed each other afterwards, cleaning away mud, or bits of grass caught in fur, which had been pushed in under a thudding assault.

Chapter Eight

DURING ONE OF THEIR MAD GAMES on the beach the otters had run to its far end, and swum into a tiny cove beneath a small waterfall. It was much smaller than the river falls, and simply spattered down over boulders from a small cliff above the beach.

The otters broke off their game of tag and went to investigate the tumbling stream. They could never resist the lure of moving water. They lolloped up to where it splashed and danced around at its base. Faces up-turned, the pair reached upon their hind legs as each tried to bite the chunks of solid water with arched necks, front paws reaching up at the cascading torrent. Then they lay on their backs in the small pool and let the jets bounce off their stomachs. After a little while one of them noticed an opening behind the fall. It was a dark space above a ledge a few feet from the base. He sat up, looking at it thoughtfully, then stretched up the rock extending his neck to peer into it. He was intrigued by the dark recess, and stepped back under the water. From there he sprang upwards, clawing at the rock. His forepaws grasped the ledge, and his hind feet scrabbled up the rock to hump him on to the ledge. Beyond the lip of rock a cavern stretched back into darkness. He disappeared into it. Meanwhile the other otter had watched his actions, and followed, immediately springing up in the same way.

The pair went hesitantly into the deep recess, snuffling suspiciously. There was no scent, save the damp smell of the cave itself. It went back four metres before rising to meet the roof, and was about a metre wide. As the floor rose it became dry, so that the back third of the cave was quite habitable.

The otters came out of the cave, and began to explore the cliff beyond the waterfall. They found that there was a way up the steeply angled cliffs in an angle between two falling bands of rock strata. Where the strata jutted out in places into a mud seam, it formed irregular steps up the incline. The otters half-ran, half-climbed their way to the top of the cliffs. There they found bracken and bilberry bushes growing. They gathered some bilberry clumps, hauling them out of the ground with back-snatching movements of their heads, while holding their jaws firmly clamped around the base of the bushes which were rooted in thin soil. They carried their prizes down the cleft into the cavern. Next they added bracken fronds as a top covering to a large bed. They were establishing a joint holt.

They discovered that at half-water the shore below the cleft was sandy, and the area proved to be a rich fishing ground on the incoming tide. Having established an extension to their range, the otters used the beach holt continuously for a week, when the weather was very bright with pale ice-blue skies and large banks of snow cloud, which processed across the distant horizon. Snow fell on the mountain behind the beach, and the river in the next bay began to swell again. During the third week in November they woke up one afternoon to a deeply chilling blast, which blew right into the holt. It was an east wind, and it began to freeze all but the most swiftly moving fresh water, so that the falls soon ran between, and added to, long icicles that hung like a curtain in front of the holt. The tide was rising to full flood, and the wind began to gather fingers of spume from the wavecrests, and hurl them into the frozen waterfall. Some of the spray penetrated to where the otters lay, and roused them.

They came out of the cave and ran to the cleft in order to climb out of the beach before high tide. They did not dare swim in the big waves that now crashed on to the shore, exploding in wind-driven spatters of icy salt spray. The force of the wind rose steadily, pushing the rising tide in faster than usual, making their escape urgent. The otters reached the cleft and began to climb it. The mud had been coated with spray, which was so salty that it resisted freezing, but the whole ascent was extraordinarily slippery. The otters grappled their way up the steep stairway, and reached the top after ten minutes of sliding, faltering ascent.

Had they stayed in the holt, they would have perished, for now the icy waves were being pushed further up the beach by the gale, and even as the otters gained the cliff-top, waves were breaking off huge icicles, as they smashed their way past the frozen waterfall to thunder into the cave itself.

As they looked back from the top of their cliff, they saw a brown flurry, as their bracken bedding was sucked out of the holt on the foaming waves.

They hurried away from the cliff edge, and then watched in wonder as the wind roared up the rock face, taking the waterfall with it. The gusts hurled the falling water upwards, back over the cliff-top in a curving jet. The stream arched back, lifted high above its bed, and fell on the cliff-top path. It continued to rain back on itself as the otters turned away to retreat inland.

They moved in short snatches, huddled to the ground, shrinking from the forces of the storm. They used every scrap of cover they could find to shelter them from the gale's relentless onslaught. They ran from tussock to tussock, and gained the slight protection of a stone wall. This brought them over the highest cliff top, above the bay to the east where the big river dropped down. They could not hear the falls until they were very close, running parallel to the river, which was foaming below them, in full spate. It carried much debris in its churning waters, even bearing away whole trees which had been knocked from the bank by raging gusts, or swept off the rocks by the charging water. The river was no place for the otters to travel in, and they kept to the high land above the gorge. Where the river opened out, it had spread beyond its banks and was beginning to flood the valley floor. The otters found their first holt was under water and travelled upstream, soaked by the heavy rain which now accompanied the storm. Anxiously they sought their next holt, so they could rest and dry out.

They came to the holt in the wood, which was on rising ground and therefore dry. At first light they wearily climbed the incline to the entrance. They went into the big chamber together and slumped down to sleep. They dried out as they slept, wedged together for warmth, and did not wake until the following afternoon when they found that the storm had moved away.

They fished in the swollen river, at the quietest of the deep pools, where the current ran less fiercely on the inside of the bend. They returned to the edge of the wood, and lay dozing on a fallen tree in the hot sun, soaking up its rays to warm their chilled bones.

The sound of a tawny owl's ghostly call, echoing in the wood, woke the recumbent otters, and they jumped down from the tree trunk. They set off together upstream to renew their acquaintance with the rest of their range.

The night's end found them five miles upstream in the head of the valley. They slept in the top holt on the river, and next evening worked their way slowly downstream to explore the area

around the highest farm. There was a stone barn on the foothills of the mountain, which was used as a store for cattle fodder. It stood in isolation, half a mile from the farm itself. Skirting the barn the otters suddenly saw a fox running towards them. It veered off and disappeared through a hedge, as it saw the otters. They went to their nearest holt as the sky lightened, slipping down behind roots at the river's edge under an overhanging elder.

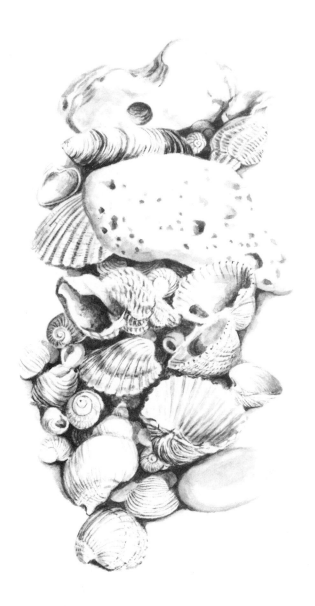

Chapter Nine

DECEMBER CAME IN with mild weather, and only the high tops of the mountains were snow covered. The days were dull and dark under overcast skies, which kept the temperature relatively mild for mid-winter. The otters took advantage of this to work their way back to the sea, where the fishing was richest. They climbed down the cleft by the stream falls, and took up residence in the cave. In the big bay next door, where the river crashed down in loud confusion on to the beach boulders below, they took to exploring the rock pools for crabs. They found a hover amongst fallen rocks, which had a narrow entrance, but opened out to give dry but draughty cover. At the least hint of danger they retreated to the hover where they could stay completely hidden. At the end of the third week in December the weather brightened for a few days and the otters took advantage of it to bask on the rocks by the entrance to their hiding place.

Up at the lowest farm there was an air of excitement as the school holidays began and the children could spend their short days at home. They planned a visit to the big fall, and decided to seek shells on the beach in the sunny afternoon. They collected the farm collie, and with shrill voices went enthusiastically down the track to the beach. The dog joined in their celebratory mood, barking and yelping as he danced around them, and led the way impatiently to the shore.

The otters heard none of this, as it was drowned in the noise of the falls. The first thing they saw was a blur of movement as the collie appeared at the top of the cliff by the falls, and began to descend the steep path that stepped down beside the boulders. They jumped up and shot inside the hover. The dog ran down the beach as the children came into sight. He picked up the scent of the otters, and instantly became alert. He quickly made his way to the hover, and pushed his nose cautiously in. The children saw him, and called out high tremulous commands, fearing for whatever was under the rocks. The dog turned a deaf ear to them and began whining and scrabbling at the entrance. The children ran up, their voices anxious as they demanded obedience from the collie. The dog's black and white paws only began to dig harder, as he barked to the children that he was on to something new. 'It might be a snake', exclaimed the younger girl fearfully, and at that they both became alarmed for the safety of the dog. This lent them new determination, and they clipped his thin lead on to his collar. Putting their arms around his body, they half lifted, half shoved him backwards. The otters, deep in the rocks, had remained silent, hoping to avoid detection, and they relaxed slightly as light came into the entrance, which had been filled with the dog's head and its barking. As soon as the children released their hold, the dog leapt forward towards the hole, intent on renewing his assault. His lead snapped tight, and he jumped round to slip his collar – but the children anticipated him and ran after him to slacken the tension.

The eldest girl became very angry. She stamped her foot and screamed at him, 'Come *here*, you bad dog – you bad, bad, horrible dog!' 'Come here at once', joined in the boy, and he scooped up the rear end of the dog, as his sister tightened its collar, so they pushed and pulled him away from the holt. The collar was now so tight that the collie's head stuck forward beyond a ruff of fur, and in a few minutes the children loosened it a notch. They were some distance from the rocks now, and the collie had become obedient once more.

The children went to look at the falls, and then, holding the dog on its lead, they gathered shells for Christmas presents, to be stuck on to boxes and round tins for Aunts and Uncles to 'put things in'.

The otters stayed deep in the hover until the falling dusk drove the children back up the cliff to plod cheerfully back to the farm. When they emerged they began hunting the beach, closely observing the scent of the children's boots, and the smell of the collie. They retraced all the wanderings of the children, huffing and stopping whenever they got a strong signal of human or dog. They ended up by the gleaming falls, satisfied that the intruders had really departed. They went to the rock pools to fish for crabs.

They felt the hover was insecure now it had been discovered by the dog, and decided to move to another part of their range.

Their sense of companionship had united them in mutual trust, and when the elder dog otter led the way out of the beach past the shining boulders by the fall, the other followed without any hesitation.

They went up the river a little way and paused in mid pace as they caught a faint trace of sound. It came from the east, and they sat still trying to hear it clearly against the background of river noise. They moved across the fields in the direction of the noise, and came to rising ground that led back from the big bay they had left. Crossing the rise they could see into the next bay. As they sat on the ridge listening, a babble of sounds drifted towards them from the fields edging the shore. They moved closer until they could make out the source of the growing waves of sound, which rose and fell irregularly. Out over the sea the sky was suddenly filled with more calls, as a flock of wild geese flew over in a vee, towards the grass sward. Already, hundred of geese were busily feeding on the eelgrass. A few stood like sentinels in the dim light, while the rest were busy, bobbing beaks down into the grass as they gobbled it up. At invervals more vees of birds showed briefly against the clouds as they circled to gauge a landing area, and then dropped down with spread feet and big, down beating wings to brake their descent. They cackled ceaselessly, defending their patch of grassy sward from neighbours in a close packed flock numbering several hundred geese.

The otters turned quickly away, back over the ridge, and went up past the farm, to a day holt they had claimed in a copse near the river. It was an old badger's sett and the otters had taken it over, since the original badger occupants had been killed. It was during a

murderous period when they were blamed for being likely to give tuberculosis to the farm cattle. They had been gassed, and were now only skeletons. The sett had been sealed with stones, but the otters had no difficulty in unblocking the tunnels, and used one of the many chambers. They chose one that was not made uncomfortable by badger bones. Above the copse the land rose to a knoll, behind which was a marshy basin. Surrounding a small pool, it was nevertheless occasionally visited by eels. The otters were checking it for prey a few days later when they heard noises from the valley below.

They looked back down to see a small party of children walking up to the neighbouring farm with a lantern on a pole to light the way. They crossed the river on a swaying footbridge suspended between tall posts on either shore, and came to the door of the farmhouse.

The watching otters heard whispered snatches of conversation, as they consulted each other. A child's throat was cleared, and they began to sing waveringly together. The singing fascinated the otters, who were too distant to worry about being chased from the farm. They sat there as the children piped out their carol, one of a dozen they had learned. A shaft of yellow light showed as the farmhouse door was drawn open, and a face peered out. Then it opened wider to admit the children. It shut with a bang – and the singing started up again in a few moments, accompanied by the deeper voices of the farmer and his wife.

The otters went on their way to seek eels. They fed well that night, catching four large eels in the pool.

Chapter Ten

DURING THE NEXT DAY it began to snow. The flakes were small at first, and melted as they touched the ground. Gradually though, they grew larger, and began to stay whole on the earth, turning the green and brown valley to a grey shade of white. That night the snow came in with renewed vigour, and built up a covering which buried the grass on the fields, drifting on to the hedges and half-drowning them. Flurries of wind began to whirl across the landscape, picking snow from the hedgestops and adding to the drifts, till they were scalloped and sculpted into hollow curving shapes along the hedgerows. Ice-encrusted hedge parsley poked above the drifts at intervals. As dawn approached the light showed brighter than usual, reflected by the snow all around. It revealed tracks of rabbit and hare, mice and shrews, badger and fox and, near the holt in the wood, of two otters, who had gone out through the snow to fish as usual, but had played on the bank, creating a snow slide. Shining fish scales sparkled in the rising sun on blue-white snow as evidence that they had fished well. Many rabbits were out in the snow, pawing away the soft powder to reveal green grass beneath.

A fox was trotting quietly on the track leading up the hill from the farm, when he spotted a rabbit feeding. He saw it through the black stems of the hedge, clearly outlined against the white snow. The rabbit was well out into the field, where the snow lay thinnest, giving the fox a chance to catch it before it regained its hole in the hedge.

The fox crouched. As his head shot forward through the base of the hedge, it passed into a wire snare set for the rabbits, but carelessly left a little too large.

Instantly the fox was brought to a painful halt. He jerked backwards, and the noose bit into his neck. With excruciating pain he jerked his head to the side, and finding himself caught, he began to run the length of the snare tether, going from side to side, shaking his head, and trying to bite at the wire which cut into him so painfully. His feet tore up the ground as he tried to obtain purchase and wrest the wire from its anchorage. It had been secured to the largest stem in the hedge, and would not loosen an inch. The wire was drawn ever tighter round his neck. As he thrashed about under the dark hedge his constricted throat made his gasps rasp as he struggled for breath. The harder he pulled the more tortured his breathing became, till he was heaving with the effort, and his breath came only in harsh gasps of hoarse coughing. The wire had torn one ear, and blood was streaked across his white neck and muzzle. His eyes were staring with fear as he continued ceaselessly to choke in the wire's steely grip. After an hour of relentless struggle he was exhausted. He collapsed on to the mud and snow beneath him and became unconscious. As he lay there, the white snow clouds of early morning crept silently over the mountain and began to smother the land in a new white blanket of big flaked soft snow. Helpless, the fox lay under the hedge, shuddering with the shock of the pain, as he drifted in and out of consciousness. As the new snow fell on him, pushed in by the mountain wind, the fox awoke with the cold. He struggled to his feet, and was jerked over by the noose, which had slipped loosely about his neck while he lay inert. He began to wrestle the wire again, choking and screaming with pain and rage. He tried biting the wire where it lead to the trunk, but only made his gums bleed as his teeth slid over the smooth meıtal, and its thin strands sliced up between them. He grew weaker after twenty minutes of continuous struggle, and collapsed eventually to drift into a coma on the snow. The icy shroud of pure white enclosed his bleeding body as he lay. His temperature dropped till it went below the point of recovery, and he died without regaining consciousness later that morning. The farmhand who had set the snares for rabbits found him a few hours later, and carried the fox back over the river. He flung it into the swollen current, and it was whirled away in a foaming pink flurry of creaming water over the rocks below. The two otters passed the spot where the fox had died, pausing to sniff at the blood, and backing off as they smelt the fox's strong scent.

The winter in late December had become gradually colder as the month drew to a close. During the first week of January it grew colder still, freezing the pond where they had found eels, and adorning the streams with fantasies of ice formations, where they ran by hedges amongst ferns and mosses which froze into beautiful shapes beside the rippling water.

The otters were coming out to hunt the river one afternoon, picking their way along the already frosty banks when they heard the distant call of another otter. It came from the head of the river up by the mountains, and echoed briefly in the frosty air. They both stood up, and the elder otter called a response – short and shrill, which was answered in turn a few seconds later by a second distant whistle.

The pair set off upriver, calling at intervals and listening to the answers growing louder as they closed the distance to the stranger. A call sounded very close to them, and they saw the stranger appear on top of the opposite riverbank. They both called at once – and dashed down into the river to greet the new otter. She, for it was a bitch otter, met them at the foot of the bank. As they scrambled out of the water she stood back a little, very still, and submitted to their inspection. Then as they chittered at her in approval, she tentatively moved her nose towards them, and exchanged scents.

They then began a mad game of tag, in which all three chased boisterously up and down the banks, and across the river.

The three of them then went off to fish. The bitch was then shown their holt in the bank. She had come through the mountains, in search of a companion, and was a young otter who had left her family range. She was about to come into season.

At the end of January her scent changed, triggering a response in both dog otters. They were normally playful, as much with her as with each other, but now their attention became

56

overbearing. They began to follow her around continually, and attempted to mate her in the river. At one point both the young dog otters resolved to attempt this at the same time, and a fight suddenly broke out. They began to scream at each other with open jaws in the swirling water. The bitch dived and shot away to the bank as they began to circle each other. Then one otter dived, followed at once by the other. They shot out up the bank, tumbling each other and biting tail and flank. The larger dog otter began to dominate the youngster. Allowing him no respite he harried and bit, and pursued him down the river bank. The young otter was unable to resist the savage onslaught, and bounded away uttering submissive whimpers and chittering with pain and fear. The big dog slowed, and watched as the youngster fled the area.

He retreated down the river, then stopped to lick his wounds. He had been bitten on his tail and flanks and on one shoulder, which was slashed open by a glancing bite. The young otter went to the holt in the wood, well away from the area occupied by his rival, and spent a day resting.

He knew he could not remain on the range without provoking further attacks, and the following night resolved to quit the area entirely.

The otter went out over the flank of the valley and looked towards the sea.

Chapter Eleven

THE OTTER DECIDED AGAINST GOING DOWN THE COAST, which was fully exposed to the bitter north-east winds that came across the sea from Greenland, bearing severe reminders of its icy origins. He turned inland and dropped into an adjoining valley, which ran towards the mountain. It held no water, and he crossed it. The next three valleys he crossed were high moorland dales, holding bog and rocky terrain before chopping steeply to the coast. He was travelling around the mountains slowly on a series of high troughs, cut by ancient glaciers in the last ice age, and bearing a grim reminder of their former state in the extreme cold of late January.

The otter ate sparsely as he travelled, and it took him two nights to discover a valley he could occupy and feed in. As he came over yet another weary mound of springy tussocky bog, he found himself looking into a dark void before him. The ground dropped steeply away below him, and the black sky gave no illumination to the valley ahead. He paused on the ice-cold squelching bog, and listened for any sound of a river. At the same time he whiffled his nose into the rising air for scent of water. His nose found it first, and then as he descended the mountainside he began to hear the river.

It was a medium-sized river, not very broad in the lower part of the valley, but deep, running through high rocky banks and rushing on down to the sea over big bars of rock which jutted out from the gorge walls.

As he approached, he heard falls, and headed inland towards the mountains. When he reached the valley floor he quickly

encountered the river. It was wider now, and shallower as the higher part of the valley levelled out to curve in a huge sweep around the base of the nearest mountain. He lay up for the day under some rocks at the water's edge. That night he travelled up the valley for five miles coming around the foot of the mountain. At first light he rested in a wood, of which there were many now, clothing the sides of the valley. They stretched down to enclose the river at times. The land became undulating and seemed gentler. He noticed that the north-east wind no longer moaned over the ground, but was gentled by the mountain baffles.

That afternoon he awoke with a new sense of purposefulness. His wounds had begun to heal, and he had found no otter spraints on the way into the valley. He began to feel hopeful once more that he might have found an unoccupied range where he could live. He slept away the morning in a bramble clump, and awoke at midday. He felt eager to explore the river.

He set out up the big valley, and at the end of the afternoon he was rising steadily higher. The valley was curving around between the mountains, following the track of a huge glacier that had carved it out ten thousand years ago. The river was running fast and wide now, over a bed of stone. Sometimes it ran on solid rocks, sculpting them into curved and lipped shapes, and at others it ran over shingle beds so that the bouncing river seemed to bubble between the stones.

At the lower end of the valley there had been a few farms amongst the woods, but now the ground was too sparse to support crops or beasts and was uncultivated.

The otter followed the winding river, until he came to its source. Quite suddenly, as he topped a crest of rising ground he found himself in a high cwm in the middle of the mountains. The area

before him was like a bowl, and it held a large lake, surrounded by a plateau of grass and bracken. At the junction of the river and the lake the otter found a spraint. It was fresh.

Two years earlier the lake and top of the river had been occupied by an elderly pair of otters, who had produced a bitch cub in the last year of their lives together. The following spring the mother had died of old age, and the succeeding bitter winter killed the old dog otter. The young bitch had remained there and now occupied the lake as her range, seldom leaving it for the river. She was nervous of contact with the farms, and had grown very secretive in her lone existence in the quiet of the mountains.

The young dog otter smelt the spraint and began to call to the other otter. His whistles echoed in the bowl of the mountains, as he listened for an answer. Across the cold night air he heard a reply. It came from the far side of the lake. He entered the water in the moonlight and swam towards the sound. He called at intervals, hanging in the water to hear the answer – and headed towards it.

The bitch was at the edge of the lake in a reed bed, apprehensive about the stranger, yet excited too by the thought that she might have another otter for company. She was fearful too, lest it be another female, who might try and drive her out.

She heard the calls coming across the lake, and waited at its edge as she answered them. In ten minutes the otter emerged close by her on the shore. She moved towards him hesitantly, and they reached their heads out to one another. Their faces moved up and around as they exchanged scents, and the inspection was then transferred to their whole bodies. When they knew they were of opposite sexes, they began to chitter at each other. The bitch rubbed her head into the dog's flank, and he rolled on to his side to flop down. She licked his face, and then buried her head beneath his to clean out his ear. He placed a waving paw on her shoulder as she moved back and forth, gently working her tongue over his fur. Then he rolled away and sprang up. She half-crouched, looking at him expectantly. A gleam appeared in his eye, and he suddenly dashed away along the reed bed.

She ran after him, and bumped his shoulder with hers as she caught up. Together they ran, shoving each other in play, and making sudden changes of direction. Their joy at finding a fellow otter was quite evident as they chased around the reed beds. Sometimes they stopped and rested, looking away as though uninterested, until a head would creep round to catch the other unawares, and a swift nudge would send them careering off again in hot pursuit.

They went fishing together in the pre-dawn glimmer. As the sun rose, they were side by side at the edge of the lake, grooming each other, and ridding their jaws of fish scale remnants. They lay down side by side and lapped at the cold water of the lake, just as the sun came over the mountains. The water reflected the yellow ball of the rising sun as it heaved itself up over the snow-capped peaks. In the rippled reflections of the glowing reeds were two whiskery otter heads, sending out circlets of water as they drank. The dog tucked his head into the water making the reflections shimmer out in golden rings through the deep blue shadows and gleaming white snows of the mirrored mountains.

Chapter Twelve

THEY SLIPPED INTO THE LAKE together, and the bitch led him across the corner of it to one of her holts. It was dug out of a turf bank hidden in the bracken, and was big enough for two or three otters, having been made by her parents. They curled up together and slept. The bitch stirred in her sleep, dreaming and chittering softly occasionally. The bigger dog just grunted as he half awoke to the comfort of her furry body, and eased his shoulders and hips into even closer contact with her back.

They were each so used to sleeping alone that it took that first day of sleep for them to settle down. While the bitch was finding it disturbing to sleep beside him, due to her nervous disposition, the dog was delighted to have the warmth and comfort of her furry form as an additional accessory to his bedding. He unashamedly used her as a warm cushion. He lay his head on her neck at times, delighting in the perfect way it fitted on to the soft pillow she provided. As their sleeps progressed over the next few days the bitch lost her restlessness, and took example from the dog otter. She too began to drape herself over him, and they ended up tangled together in mutual bliss.

The bitch had confined her range mainly to the lake and its surrounding bowl, seldom venturing down river towards the farms, and she was only disturbed very occasionally by the landowner.

The dog was of a much more fearless disposition and began to make forays down the river. The bitch had two holts near the lake and one at the top of the river, and she took the dog to all three in turn. She took him all around the lake in the next two nights, and showed him her routes up the streams that fed the bowl. On the third night the dog otter led her, for a change, and took her past the riverhead holt down towards the middle of the river where the woodland clothed its banks, and was infiltrated by cultivated farmland.

Emboldened by his confidence the bitch explored the river with him. Each new bend was thoroughly investigated, and their progress was slow. They frequently crossed the river going out over the banks. They poked their muzzles into every interesting hole, clump or bush by the banks. First one otter, usually the dog, would pause to snuffle and push with his nose then the bitch would join him, nudging his head aside as she tried to discover what was so interesting. They rested at intervals, napping for an hour before continuing their explorations.

Towards the end of the night they came to the second of the wooded sections of the river, and decided to make a holt. They found a large sycamore at the water's edge whose roots sprang out from the eroded bank on to the thin mud beach at the water's edge. The river, often in spate, had washed out a large area up under the tree, exposing thin sandy soil around its roots. The otters proceeded to dig this area out, tunnelling inwards and upwards. They curved their entrance tunnel, and excavated a chamber angled back towards the river so it ran parallel to it. The holt was only just big enough for them to lie side by side, and they spent the dawn tunnelling back from the river towards the chamber. They made the second tunnel from between the roots that stretched away from the tree and down to the mud. They broke back into the chamber at dawn, thus creating an escape tunnel. Then they hurried out to clean up with a brief swim. They hunted hungrily in the brightening sunrise, and carried two sizeable roach to the beach, where they lay half in the water to eat them. They glanced around as the light spilled about them, and after a hurried roll and wipe on the grass above, disappeared into the holt.

When they awoke, it was to a bright February afternoon. Reflected light from the river dappled the entrance tunnel with lines of pale light, and the smell of warm mud drifted into their noses. A spider was weaving its web across the new hole, and it shone in the light from beyond.

First one, then a second bewhiskered face poked enquiringly out from the sycamore roots, as the two otters blinked their way into the afternoon brilliance outside.

Pale blue sky was reflected in the shining ripples of the river as it ran by them. The bonus of a sunny day this far into winter had roused the birds and hibernating insects into a flurry of activity.

65

Finches and robins, wrens and bluetits all sang noisily in the saplings at the edge of the wood, finding unexpectedly easy prey, or soaking up warmth from the sun. A tree creeper was slowly spiralling up an oak, gathering insects as they emerged into the false spring.

The bitch otter left the holt first, and stood quietly amongst the roots listening to the river. The bolder dog pushed past her impatiently, and slid into the river. She shuddered, shocked by his incautious exit, but followed him anyway. Two vee wakes moved side by side as the otters crossed the river. They turned back as they neared the far shore, and began to work their way down the river-banks occasionally crossing the deep slow pools in search of fish.

The dog otter caught a grayling basking near the surface, and the bitch caught another a few minutes later. They ate them on the bank in the warm sun.

Continuing downstream they suddenly saw a white flash ahead of them. It was a dipper, bobbing on a rock in the shallows. He spotted the otters and vanished, turning his back on them and blending with the river. Keeping low over the water he flew straight downstream, merging into the shadows of the banks.

They continued their meandering progress, searching the banks and water thoroughly to become fully acquainted with the extension of their range.

As the sun was setting they fished again. A shoal of grayling was lying on the surface in one of the deep pools. Their gleaming scales flashed in the dying light as one or two occasionally darted away. The otters spotted them from the bank above, and moved back out of sight. They ran along the bank, and entered the river ten metres downstream. By this ruse they were able to approach the basking shoal of grayling from below, disguising their own pressure waves in

the rippling current and hiding their smell, which was carried away from the fish. They approached a metre below the surface, seeing the fish silhouetted above them against the bright red glowing water. They shot upwards together, and simultaneously burst through the river's surface, each with a grayling in their jaws. The dog otter reached the bank first, and as the bitch followed him up the same slope, he turned and growled at her through a mouthful of fish. The bitch hesitated, then turned aside across the slope, to reach the top of the bank two metres away. The dog kept raising his head between bites, glancing at the bitch and whickering a warning to keep away. She ignored him and chewed her way through her own fish.

He finished his meal and began moving towards her. She sensed his intention to muscle in on her fish too, and she ran off with the last part of the grayling in her mouth. She fled along the bank, till she spotted a hawthorn tree with a cage of roots where it had previously grown on a mound of earth. She shot into the stronghold and faced the dog otter as he came up. She hastily took a bite as he approached, and then looked at him, with a malevolent gleam in her eye. He hesitated while she swallowed the mouthful, and began a tirade of abuse. She uttered a chattering rising note that ended, as the dog moved tentatively forward still, in a high short scream. The big otter stepped back a pace, and she quickly took another bite. He looked on. His tongue flicked idly round his gums, and he slumped down to watch her eat.

She kept on glancing at him as she finished her fish. He pretended he did not notice, and licked his paws clean of fish scales. One got stuck under his nostril, and he snorted and shook his head till it flew out. Then he lay on his back and licked his white chest, glancing sideways at her frequently. She stopped chewing and stared at him, stock still, and dared him to even think about pinching her meal. When she had finished the fish she cleaned her paws and came out to rub her jaws on the grass. She came over to the supine dog and rolled into his side, so they lay together, upside down, side by side on the grass. Long shadows reached over the river as the sun disappeared behind the trees. The drop in temperature as the shadows touched the otters galvanised them into action. They moved off into the dusk, like shadows themselves, flitting among the banks and boulders of the riverside.

Over the next three nights they thoroughly investigated the river as far as the sea, and during the week that they took to arrive back at the lake, they converted or excavated four more holts. They had doubled their range at the instigation of the bold male, who was not content with the relative monotony, secure though it was, of the lake and its surrounding area.

Chapter Thirteen

FEBRUARY ENDED IN MILDER WEATHER, but contrary March brought a brief spell of snow storms and frosts that shook the fist of departing winter. Warmer winds blew into the mountain bowl and the otters noticed the smell of spring on its breath. The lake and the farms were part of a huge private estate, and the otters were rarely disturbed as they roamed the river and lake range.

At the end of the month skeins of geese flew across the bowl. Their soft chatter of honking was faintly heard by the otters on several nights as the big flocks departed their winter feeding grounds by the sea and headed for the arctic summer.

The bitch otter felt suddenly secure in the company of her companion. He was now a well-muscled, fully-grown otter of seventeen months, and his bold attitude to life had given her a degree of confidence in their joint safety.

The spring weather, and the sudden burst of new life all around affected her too. She first noticed it as she became intensely irritable, and then she realised she was coming into season.

The dog otter, always companionable, now became utterly attentive to her every waking moment. During their boisterous play, after fishing, he began to pursue her with great persistence, to the point where she became very cross with him. Suddenly as she was pressed too hard, she would turn and lunge at him, fangs bared, and a hoarse scream on her lips. He would stop – abashed at this crushing response, and wander after her looking downcast till her temper improved, and they played once more.

This pattern of behaviour lasted for four nights during which time the dog otter became very exhausted. His ceaseless attempts to woo the bitch took their toll. His eye acquired a wild and desperate look, and he panted as he was briefly repulsed at intervals.

On the fifth day when he awoke in the late afternoon, he lay beside the bitch, licking her rear quarters and waiting to be cursed. The bitch woke immediately and rose to push past him out of the holt. To his surprise he found her waiting for him as he emerged into the daylight. Then she dashed off down the mud beach, and raced up the bank around the roots of the big sycamore. He set off after her as usual, and chased her around the saplings along the river bank. Then she dived into the river with a huge splash, which he echoed at once as he hit the water behind her. They torpedoed away below the surface as he tried to catch her, and she fled up the far bank. She began a game of hide and seek with him among the bushes on the far bank. They streaked over the uneven ground, and slid under bushes as she tried to outwit him. When she hid successfully she soon peeped out, to call at him, and shoot away as he discovered her. She led him back and forth along the bushes, and then she ambushed him. As he came charging after her, she quickly spun and leapt sideways. As he passed she gave him a light nip on his flank. He braked in a welter of torn grass, and leapt after her. She vanished into a clump of tall dry grass, only to reappear by the river. She glanced back as his form scythed through the grasses, then dived into the river. Their pursuit continued under water. The surface of the river boiled as they rose head to hear baring their mouths in a laugh rather than a snarl. They grappled and rolled together in the river. The tumbling pursuit took them once more out of the river. Their shaking bodies covered the banks with spray as they momentarily rid themselves of surplus weight, then went charging off at full tilt along the bank. They rolled each other over, legs flying, grasping for purchase as they wriggled upright. For ten more minutes this mad chase led them in and out of the water. Then, as though having exhausted all sense of aggression, they clasped each other and coupled in the swirling river, that rocked them as they drifted down its slow current. Afterwards, loosely coiled round one another, they lay exhausted in the river, letting it wash them downstream. It moved them in a slow spiral past the holt, and they lay limply blissful for a few minutes. They were jerked out of their reverie by the kik-kik call of a kingfisher. He rocketed past them, his brilliant plumage flashing as it caught the light, and then was gone. His calls continued up the river for a few moments, ceasing when he reached his fishing perch on a twig just above the water.

The river gurgled as it neared the bend, and began to run over a shingle bank. The otters disentangled and swam a circle to head back up to the holt. In the late afternoon a cow lowed on the mountainside, its call echoing in the still air. The squabble of roosting birds filled the riverbanks with shrill sound, as the sunset began to weave its few minutes of magic by the otters' holt.

The otters climbed from the water and lay on the bank above their holt. As dusk arrived it brought with it a soft whoo – whiwhoooo. The female tawny owl from the wood behind the holt was calling up her mate. He answered from across the river with a keewik cry. Then he flew over to join her and they sat shoulder to shoulder on an oak branch leaning into each other's soft brown, speckled sides.

The bitch otter rolled over and turned around to face the dog. Gently she licked his face, her head bobbing as her tongue methodically rubbed at his ears, then his neck, and finally his eyes. He groaned contentment, and nuzzled her affectionately. Then they rose together, and their two humping shapes melted into the dark river as they went fishing.

In late August the owner of the land made one of his rare visits to the high lake, to watch Red-Throated Divers which nested there each summer. As he sat watching the shore with binoculars, his attention was diverted by a ripple to his right. Swinging the glasses towards the disturbance he was both astonished and delighted to observe an otter swimming out from the reeds. To his amazement she was followed by her cub. She lingered in the water, allowing its anxious, bobbing form to catch her up. The cub took her tail in its mouth, and together they moved out over the lake in a string, joined together head to tail like a single long animal.

Suddenly the bitch noticed his shape, and huffed in alarm. Mother and cub dived together, leaving only ripples to give credence to what he had seen.

The man returned a few days later, and crept up on the cub at play in the mouth of the lake. To his great joy he saw both dog and bitch otter lying together on the bank above. He watched quietly for half an hour, and then silently retreated without disturbing the family.